HOORAY FOR HAT!

Words and pictures by

Brian Won

Houghton Mifflin Harcourt
Boston • New York

For Leny and Charlie

When Elephant woke up, he was very grumpy.

The doorbell rang.

Elephant stomped down the stairs.

"GO AWAY!

I'M GRUMPY!"

There was a present on the doorstep!

Elephant unwrapped the box.

It was hard to stay grumpy now.

"HOORAY FOR HAT!"

Elephant cheered.

"I will show Zebra!"

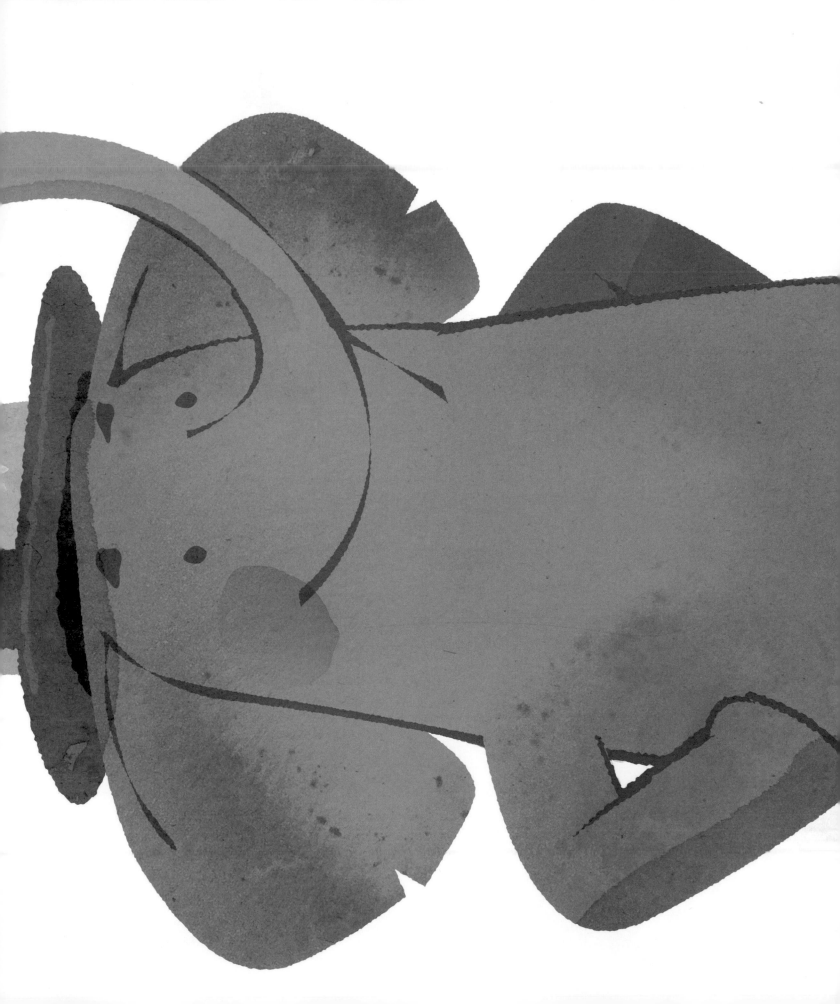

But Zebra did not want to look at any hats.

"GO AWAY!
I'M GRUMPY!"

So Elephant gave Zebra a hat.

Zebra smiled. They both cheered,

"HOORAY

FOR HAT!

Let's show Turtle!"

But Turtle would not come out of his shell.

"GO AWAY!

I'M GRUMPY!"

Elephant gave Turtle a hat too.

Turtle smiled. They all cheered,

"HOORAY FOR HAT!

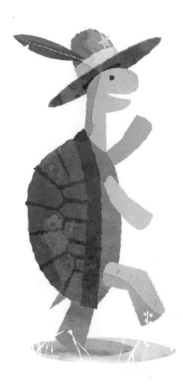

Let's show Owl!"

But Owl did not want to see them or their hats.

"GO AWAY! I'M GRUMPY!"

Elephant gave Owl a hat too.
Owl smiled. They all cheered,

"HOO-
HOO-
HOORAY
FOR HAT!"

Elephant, Zebra, Turtle, and Owl
marched down the road to show Lion.

ORAY

FOR HAT!"

But Lion did not want any visitors.

"GO AWAY!
I'M GRUMPY!"

Elephant gave Lion a hat too. But Lion was still sad. "I love this hat. But I can't cheer while our friend Giraffe is not feeling well. What can we do?"

So Elephant, Zebra, Turtle, Owl,
and Lion made a surprise for Giraffe.

They all marched to Giraffe's home.
On the way, Lion started to feel better.
And soon . . .

. . . Giraffe felt better too.